To my wonderful family for their support and
to our little buddy Walter.

Printed in the United States of America by CreateSpace,
an Amazon.com company.

Library of Congress ISBN-13: 978-1511730501
ISBN-10: 1511730501

Book Design by Peg Bala

Meet

Walter

...the Kids Named Him!

Written By Caroline Kiggins
Illustrated by Tracey Hudson Countz

Caroline Kiggins

Meet Walter

This is the story of how Walter got his unusual name.

It begins when Walter was a puppy, still living with his mother, father, brothers and sisters. He would dream about the day he would be adopted by a loving family that would give him a wonderful name at last.

Walter's brother got the great news one day that he was going to be adopted by a family and he would be going to his new home soon. This made Walter very sad as he wanted a new home too, and he was going to miss his brother.

When Walter's brother arrived at his new home the neighbors came out to greet him. One neighbor, who was feeling a bit blue because another one of her children had left for college, fell in love with the sweet puppy. She asked if there were any more Bichon puppies that needed homes. The answer was "Yes!"

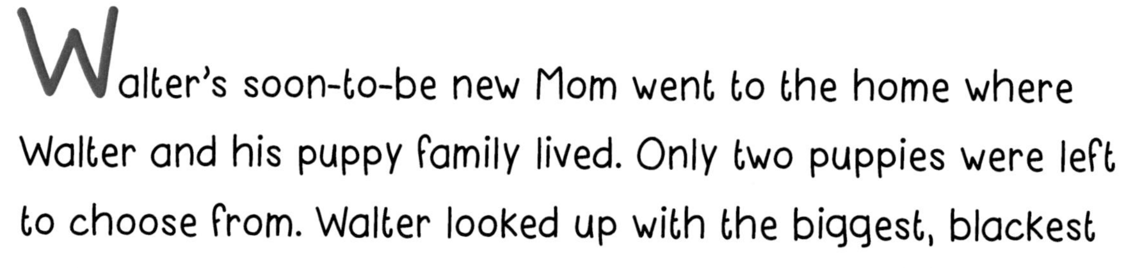

Walter's soon-to-be new Mom went to the home where Walter and his puppy family lived. Only two puppies were left to choose from. Walter looked up with the biggest, blackest Bichon eyes and it was decided in an instant that Walter would be adopted too. His new owner was overjoyed to have a new furry puppy to love and take care of.

Off they all went in their great big car that stopped in the driveway of Walter's new home. Though he had no name yet, Walter felt sure it would be a great one. They are so nice, and what a perfect looking new place to live in, he thought with pride.

Much to Walter's surprise when he hopped out of the car he thought he saw his brother across the street. The puppy and his mom crossed the street and as the other puppy got closer Walter realized it was his puppy brother! The two Moms chatted and cooed over Walter while the two puppies ran around in circles looking like one giant cotton ball. Walter's brother did not have a name yet either.

After such an eventful day, it was time to rest. Night had come and it was time for all to go to sleep. Walter's new family created a space just for Walter. Walter's new kennel was a place to keep him safe from harm and with a blanket over the top Walter thought it looked like a cozy cave. Inside was another blanket for Walter to snuggle with and an alarm clock! Walter didn't need the clock to tell time; instead it reminded him of his Mom's heartbeat and made him relax.

Walter was so sleepy he didn't think about anything except what his new name would be, in fact, he dreamt all night about it. Would it be Lucky or Snowball or Buddy? He really liked Snowball. Walter fell asleep, softly saying to himself over and over again, "Snowball, good boy Snowball, come." He crossed his paws in anticipation of being named Snowball.

Walter just loved all the attention he was getting, but still no name! They were all talking about it, they hadn't forgotten, they just hadn't decided. Walter beamed when he heard them say what an adorable puppy he was, and that he should have a very proper name. After all, he was so snowy white and as fluffy as the down feathers of a baby duck. Walter was still dreaming of Snowball.

The next morning after a wonderful night of sleep, the whole family gathered in the kitchen by Walter's den. All the kids were home for the weekend and they decided Walter should have a human name. They felt he had so much personality a puppy name wouldn't do him justice. One son thought maybe Jacques would suit him since Bichons have a French heritage. Whispering to each other, the kids yelled out a variety of "human" names. Then it happened, one daughter yelled out "Walter" and everyone laughed. And so it was decided that day, "Walter" was the fluffy little puppy's name.

Walter!

W-a-l-t-e-r??? Walter wasn't so sure about his name. When he saw his own reflection in the glass storm door he did not think he looked like a Walter, not yet anyway. What he saw was certainly a "Snowball." But Walter was sure his family knew what was best, his mother said they would know the right name. And so, Walter's life began with his new family.

Walter started to feel at home with his new family but they sure made funny sounds when they talked to him. They used high pitched voices when they told him how cute he was. It seemed a little odd, and made him think of other puppies howling. Walter concluded that is how people expressed their love. And Walter sure liked all the love he was getting, so he decided he could get used to that!

Weeks passed and life was like a wonderful dream of eating, playing and daydreaming. On this particular day, Walter woke up, ate his breakfast and waited to go out and play. But that didn't happen. Today was the day Mom was to take him to the vet for his puppy check-up. This was a complete surprise to Walter and he was clearly a little scared about his first trip to the doctor. Thankfully Mom was going with him, which made him feel safe.

As they sat in the waiting room, Mom explained the doctor was just going to give him a check-up to make sure he was well. She explained to Walter that veterinarians love all dogs and that they went to school to learn how to help dogs get well if they were sick or had gotten hurt. They were very smart and good.

As they waited, Walter imagined himself in a white lab coat like the doctor's and helping one of the pets in the waiting room. Knowing now that the doctor only wants to help animals, Walter was no longer afraid, and thought when he grew up he would help dogs and people, which made him feel safe.

Walter was just about to examine his patient's paw, when the nurse's voice broke into his daydream, announcing that they could see the doctor now.

Protect your pet...
FLEE AWAY RX
APRIL
1 2 3 4
5 6 7 8 9 10 11
12 13 14 15 16 17 18
19 20 21 22 23 24 25
26 27 28 29 30

The doctor asked Walter's Mom what they named the new puppy. Walter's Mom said "Walter" and smiled. The doctor asked how the family came to choose such a proper name for such a cute fluffy dog who looked like a little snowball. Truthfully, Walter's Mom said, "The kids named him!" She explained they wanted their friend to have a proper good name, one that people would respect for they believed Walter would grow up to be a very smart dog.

Walter grinned from ear-to-ear hearing that, sat bravely for his exam, and received great praise from his new friend, the doctor.

Since that first visit, time and time again, Mom would be asked the same question the doctor asked that day. She'd smile and simply answer in truth and one breath, "Walter, the kids named him." Most people would chuckle upon hearing the name and would immediately look at Walter as though to see if the name suited him.

Walter grew up to be a very impressive fellow. He grew to love his name and his family, and they shared may wonderful times playing and going for long walks.

Walter especially loved play dates with his doggie brother across the street that was by now named Dusty.

Walter and Dusty still loved running around together looking like a giant white fluff ball romping through the yard.

Walter was so happy he was chosen by such a kind family and that he was able to live so close to his puppy brother, Dusty.

Whether you decide to purchase a new pet or take advantage of the wonderful opportunities shelters offer, remember a pet is a big commitment. When purchasing a pet from a respected breeder, it's a good idea to see at least one of the parents of the puppy or kitten to see how they interact with their human family. Choose a pet whose temperament, size, and personality will be a good fit for your family. A little bit of research can help you realize if your family is ready for the responsibility of a pet addition and the financial responsibility as well. Pet ownership can enrich your life as well as your pet's!

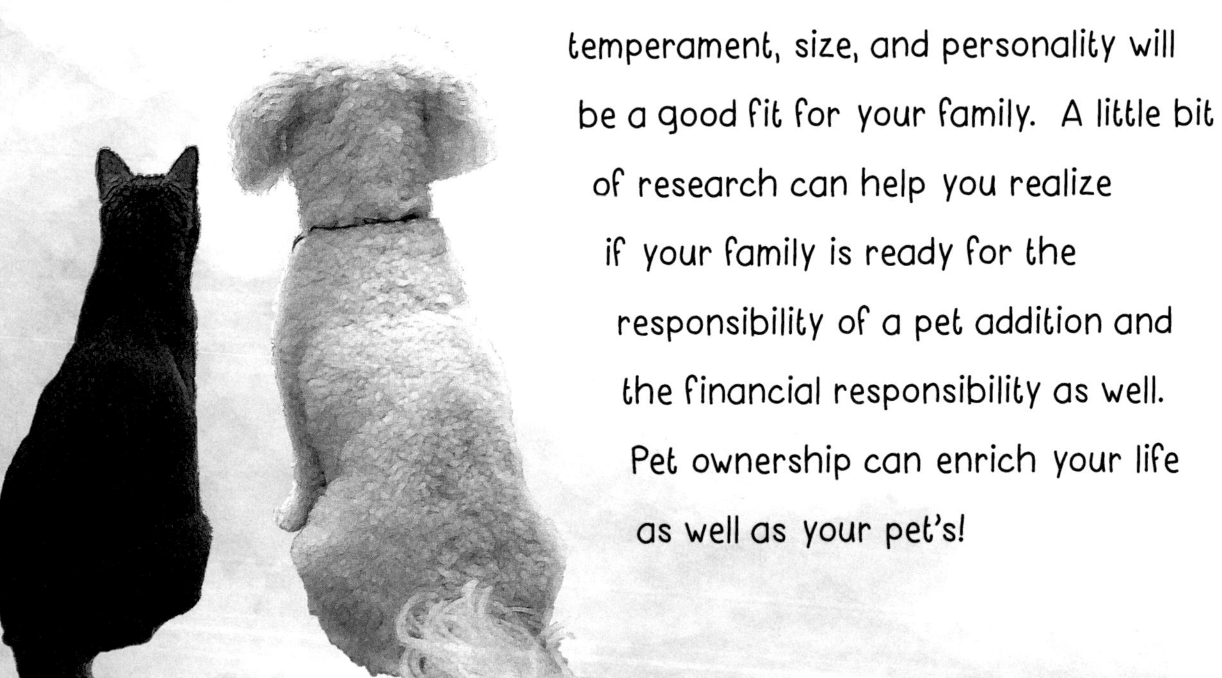

Made in the USA
Middletown, DE
27 July 2015